Maggie
Can't Wait

Published in Canada by Fitzhenry & Whiteside,
195 Allstate Parkway, Markham, Ontario L3R 4T8

Published in the United States by Fitzhenry & Whiteside,
311 Washington Street, Brighton, Massachusetts 02135

www.fitzhenry.ca   godwit@fitzhenry.ca

10 9 8 7 6 5 4 3 2 1

Library and Archives Canada Cataloguing in Publication

Wishinsky, Frieda
Maggie can't wait / by Frieda Wishinsky ; illustrated by Dean Griffiths.
Interest age level: 5-8.
ISBN 978-1-55455-103-3
I. Griffiths, Dean, 1967- II. Title.
PS8595.I834M33 2008   jC813'.54   C2008-902524-5

**U.S. Publisher Cataloging-in-Publication Data
(Library of Congress Standards)**

Wishinsky, Frieda.
Maggie can't wait / Frieda Wishinsky ; illustrated by Dean Griffiths.
[32] p. : col. ill. ; cm.
Summary: Maggie can't wait to show her friends the picture of her soon-to-be
adopted sister, but she is mortified by their reaction. If the baby is as ugly as they say,
maybe Maggie's parents shouldn't adopt her. Maggie may learn
that beauty is in the eye of the beholder.
ISBN-13: 978-1-55455-103-3
1. Adoption – Juvenile fiction. 2. Sisters – Juvenile fiction. I. Griffiths, Dean. II. Title.
[E] dc22   PZ7.W574Ma 2008

Fitzhenry & Whiteside acknowledges with thanks the Canada Council for the Arts,
and the Ontario Arts Council for their support of our publishing program. We acknowledge
the financial support of the Government of Canada through the Book Publishing
Industry Development Program (BPIDP) for our publishing activities.

 Canada Council   Conseil des Arts    ONTARIO ARTS COUNCIL
for the Arts   du Canada   CONSEIL DES ARTS DE L'ONTARIO

Design by Wycliffe Smith Design Inc.

Printed in China
The illustrations in this book are rendered in watercolour & pencil crayon.

Maggie
Can't Wait

by Frieda Wishinsky

Illustrated by Dean Griffiths

Fitzhenry & Whiteside

To Maggie's friend, Ann Featherstone
Frieda

For my beautiful, little Holly
Dean

Maggie jumped out of bed. She picked up the
new baby's picture and danced around her room.
Tomorrow she'd finally have a sister!

"She's wonderful!" everyone would coo when Maggie wheeled her sister down the street.

"She's sweet!" they'd sing when Maggie took her to the park.

"She's beautiful!" they'd exclaim when
Maggie brought her to school.

On the way to school, Maggie told her mom,
"I can't wait to show Sam her picture. I can't wait to
show everyone."

Maggie skipped down the hall into her classroom.
She sat down beside Sam.

"Who has something to share today?" asked Ms. Brown.

Maggie's hand flew up.

"Come on up, Maggie," said Ms. Brown.

Maggie marched to the front of the class.

"This is my new baby sister," Maggie
announced, holding the baby's picture high so the
class could see. "We're picking her up tomorrow
at the adoption agency. And she's beautiful and
wonderful and sweet."

"Oh yeah," snickered Kimberly.
Maggie ignored her.

But at recess, Kimberly tapped Maggie on the shoulder. "You think you're special because you have a new sister. Well, you're not. And besides, your new sister is ugly."

"She is not," said Maggie. "She's beautiful and wonderful and sweet. Right, Sam?"

"I-I-I," stammered Sam.

"See?" said Kimberly. "Even your best friend thinks your new sister is ugly."

Kimberly tossed her hair and walked off.

"You don't think she's ugly, do you, Sam?" Maggie asked.

"W-w-well," stammered Sam. "Her n-nose *is*
a little squished. Her ears *are* a little big. And
her f-f-face *is* a little wrinkled. But she might
look a lot better later."

"How can you say that?" cried Maggie.

Maggie ran to the school steps and sniffed back her tears. Why didn't Sam like her new sister? What if no one liked her new sister?

What if everyone laughed when Maggie wheeled her down the street?

What if everyone covered their eyes when Maggie took her to the park?

What if everyone snickered when Maggie brought her to school?

"We're having a Welcome Baby party tomorrow,"
Maggie's mom told her that evening. "Grandma, Grandpa,
Sam, and his parents are coming."

Maggie slumped on her bed.

She'd rather eat a barrel of worms than see that new baby's big ears tomorrow.

She'd rather be dumped into a garbage can full of rotten eggs than see that new baby's wrinkled face tomorrow.

She'd rather clean up after a hundred elephants
than see that new baby's squished nose tomorrow.

Maybe her parents could pick up a different baby.
Maybe they could find one with a little round nose.
Or one with tiny, perfect ears.
Or one without
a single wrinkle
on her face.

But Maggie knew they
wouldn't pick another baby.
They wanted this baby.

The next morning, Maggie and her parents drove to the adoption agency.

Maggie's parents rushed over to the crib where the new baby was sleeping.

"She's beautiful!" they sang. "She's as beautiful as a rose, and that's what we'll call her. Come see her, Maggie."

Maggie trudged over to the crib. She peeked in. *Oh no!* she thought.

Rose's nose was as flat as
a squished bug. Rose's ears were
as big as a donkey's. Rose's face was
as wrinkled as an old shoe.

Rose slept all the way home.

Rose was still asleep when Grandma and
Grandpa and Sam and his parents came over.
Everyone crowded around to see her.

"Ooh! Ahh!" they cooed. "What a beautiful baby!"

But Sam didn't coo. Sam didn't *ooh* or *ahh*.
Sam didn't say anything.

"Let's have cake and ice cream in the dining room," said Maggie's mom. Everyone hurried to the dining room.

Everyone except Maggie

Maggie ran to her room and flopped down on her bed. Then she heard a cry. It came from the baby's room.

Maggie ran in and peeked into the crib. The baby's cheeks were wet with tears.

"Hi, Rose," said Maggie, and she tickled her toes. Rose wiggled and squiggled.

"Don't cry," said Maggie, and she wiped away the baby's tears. Rose smiled at Maggie. Her smile lit up the room.

"Sam! Sam! Come quick," called Maggie.

"Look!" said Maggie. Sam looked into the crib.
Rose smiled at Sam.

"Hey!" said Sam. "She likes me! I—"

"Like her nose?" said Maggie.

"Yes," said Sam.

"And her ears?" said Maggie.

"Yes," said Sam.

"And her face?" said Maggie.

"Yes," said Sam. "I like your sister."

"Me, too!" said Maggie.